The Buddy Files

# THE CASE OF THE
# MIXED-UP
# MUTTS

Dori Hillestad Butler

Pictures by Jeremy Tugeau

Albert Whitman & Company
Chicago, Illinois

Library of Congress Cataloging-in-Publication Data

Butler, Dori Hillestad.
The Buddy files: the case of the mixed-up mutts / by Dori Hillestad Butler ;
illustrated by Jeremy Tugeau.
p. cm.
Summary: While attending obedience class with his new humans, Buddy the dog
helps solve a mystery involving two pugs that were switched at the dog park.
[1. Dogs—Fiction. 2. Mistaken identity—Fiction. 3. Mystery and detective stories.]
I. Tugeau, Jeremy, ill. II. Title. III. Title: Case of the mixed-up mutts.
PZ7.B9759Bul 2010
[Fic]—dc22
2009038724

Printed in China
13 12 11 10 9 HH 20 19 18 17 16

The design is by Nick Tiemersma.

For more information about Albert Whitman & Company,
visit our web site at www.albertwhitman.com.

For Dave, who *really* needs a dog.

# Table of Contents

# 1
## Who Am I?

Hello! My name is...

Hmm, what *is* my name?

I always thought my name was King. That's what Kayla and her mom and dad call me. Kayla says I am the King of Crime-solving. I LOVE solving crimes. It's my favorite thing!

I haven't seen Kayla and her family for a long time. Kayla's mom is in a place called the National Guard. That means she's far away from home, but she's okay. I don't know where Kayla and Dad are. What happened to them is a mystery. A mystery I am still trying to solve.

Here is what I know about the Case of the Missing Family:

- 🐾 Kayla and her dad went to Grandma's house in Springtown.
- 🐾 They left me at Barker Bob's.
- 🐾 They never came back.
- 🐾 Our neighbor, Mr. Sanchez, picked me up from Barker Bob's.
- 🐾 I stayed at Mr. Sanchez's for a while, then Uncle Marty came and took me to the P-o-U-N-D.

🐾 My people would never let
    me go to the P-O-U-N-D.
🐾 Something bad has happened
    to Kayla and Dad.

While I was at the P-O-U-N-D,
I accidentally adopted some new
people. Their names are Connor
and Mom. They're new around here.
They don't know Kayla and her mom
and dad. And they don't know that
Kayla, Mom, and Dad are my other
people.

Here are some good things about
going to live with Connor and his
mom:

🐾 They have good food and
    cool toys.

🐾 They just put a doggy door in their house. Now I can go outside and come back in whenever I want to.

🐾 When Connor's mom isn't looking, Connor lets me sleep in his bed.

🐾 Connor and his mom live in the house behind Kayla's. That means I can keep a nose on the place. I will be the first to know if my people come back.

Here are some bad things about going to live with Connor and his mom:

🐾 They are getting attached
   to me.

🐾 I am getting attached
   to them.

🐾 I don't know what will happen
   when Kayla and her dad come
   back.

Will I go back to Kayla's house or will I stay here with Connor and his mom?

While I am thinking about these things, the back door at my new house opens. Connor and Mom step outside, and Mom pats her legs. "Buddy, come!" she calls.

Buddy is the word that Connor and his mom call me. Buddy is another word for friend.

"It's time to go to obedience school," Mom says.

I LOVE obedience school. It's my favorite thing! I zoom across the yard, my tail spinning 'round and 'round behind me. Mom snaps a leash to my collar.

"Let's go to the car, Buddy," Connor says.

I LOVE riding in the car. It's my favorite thing!

No, wait. Obedience school is my favorite thing. If Mom and Connor pass obedience school, they will take me to a different kind of school. The kind Kayla went to. I wonder if it's even the *exact same school* that Kayla went to. If it is, maybe I'll see some of her friends there. Maybe they'll talk about what happened to her.

At the very least, I'll make new friends at that school. I LOVE new friends. They're my favorite thing!

But solving crimes is my favorite thing, too.

*I'm so confused!* No wonder I don't know my own name.

Here's a problem with humans: Sometimes it's hard to tell what they really want you to do. They may say "sit" with their mouths, but the rest of their bodies say "jump on me." Then they wonder why we jump on them.

I think this is why some humans

go to obedience school. *Obedience* is a big word. It means humans learning to say what they mean.

Some humans are easier to train than others.

I don't mean to brag, but Connor and his mom are the best-trained humans in the class. When Mom says "sit," she says it with her mouth, her hands, and her whole entire body. When Connor says "down," he says it with his mouth, his hands, and his whole entire body.

I do whatever Connor and his mom tell me to do at obedience school. Then something strange happens: I get a liver treat. I don't know why I'm the one who gets the treat instead of Connor or Mom, but I'm not complaining. I LOVE liver treats. They're my favorite food!

I feel bad for the pug who stands beside me in the circle. I don't know the pug's name, but her human's name is Kathy. Kathy is not as smart as my humans are.

Kathy says, "Sit!" with her mouth, but the rest of her body says, "Go over there and say hello to that black Lab across the circle."

The pug doesn't know what to do. So she just stands there and looks at Kathy. She waits for Kathy to give her another signal.

"I said, *sit!*" Kathy says. Louder this time. But the rest of her body says, "Lie down."

The pug drops to her belly. I would

do the same thing. What a human says with her body is usually more important than what she says with her mouth.

Kathy smells frustrated. But I bet the pug is even more frustrated than Kathy is.

I sniff. No, the pug isn't frustrated. She's just sad.

The alpha human at obedience school says to Kathy, "You need to make sure you have your dog's attention. Say your dog's name when you give a command."

"I can't," Kathy says with her hands on her hips. She turns away from her dog. "I don't know what this dog's real name is."

The other dogs and I shift around

uncomfortably. How does a human forget her own dog's name?

I think the alpha human in this class is wondering the same thing. "What do you mean?" she asks.

Kathy looks down at the floor. "I don't expect you to believe me," she says softly. "The police didn't."

*Police?* "Why would your human call the police?" I ask the pug.

The pug sniffs the floor. She doesn't seem to want to talk about it.

"This isn't my dog," Kathy says. "She may look like Muffin from a distance, but she's not. My Muffin has a darker nose and a wider face. And she doesn't act anything like this dog." She makes it sound as if this dog is acting really bad.

Kathy goes on. "I think Muffin was switched with another dog."

"What?" Rosie, the Westie, sits up.

"I don't believe it." Shadow, the black Lab, shakes his head.

"Bad human," Ike, the boxer, says. "Why would she make up such a story?"

I sniff Kathy's feet. "I don't know," I tell the other dogs. "Sniff the human. She might be telling the truth." Most dogs can tell when humans are lying and when they're telling the truth.

The other dogs' noses twitch.

"I can't tell," says Rosie. "She could be telling the truth. She could also be lying."

The pug speaks up at last. "She's telling the truth. Her dog Muffin and I left the dog park with the wrong humans."

# 2
# The Real Mystery

The pug's name is Jazzy.

"What happened, Jazzy?" Ike asks while the humans are busy cleaning up after class. "How did you and Muffin end up with the wrong humans?"

Jazzy sits beside us. "Owen—that's my human—saw Muffin doing a bunch of tricks at the dog park," she says with a sniff. "Muffin can roll over and dance on her hind legs; she can even play

pat-a-cake." Jazzy looks at the floor.
"I don't do any of that stuff. I think
Owen decided he'd rather have Muffin
than me. So... he took her."

Shadow's eyes grow dark. "What
do you mean, he took her?"

"He picked her up and walked out
of the dog park with her," Jazzy says.

It's hard to imagine a human
doing such a thing. "Maybe he didn't
know he had the wrong dog," I say.
"Did you just get this human?"

"No, I've had him for a long time,"
Jazzy says. "And Owen knew what he
was doing. When no one was looking,
he twisted Muffin's tag off her collar
and stuck it in his pocket."

We all gasp.

"Then he took my tag off my collar

and clipped it to Muffin's collar," Jazzy goes on. "And off they went. With Owen pretending Muffin was his dog."

"But that's dognapping!" Rosie cries. "Didn't anyone try to stop him? Didn't you? Didn't Muffin?"

"How could we?" Jazzy asks. "Owen is bigger than we are. I tried to follow him, but he closed the gate on me. And Muffin yelled, 'Help! Help! This isn't my human!' But no one helped."

"You and Muffin should have bitten your human," Rosie says. "That would have stopped him."

"It's not okay to bite humans," I tell Rosie.

"It is if the human tries to dognap you," Rosie argues.

"No," I growl at her. "It's *never* okay."

Rosie backs away from me. "Well, what about Muffin's human?" she asks Jazzy. "Why didn't she stop Owen?"

"Kathy wasn't at the dog park," Jazzy says. "She was sick that day, so she paid a neighbor boy to take Muffin for a walk. She didn't even know that the boy took Muffin to the dog park."

"Why didn't that boy stop Owen?" Ike asks.

Jazzy sadly shakes her head. "He didn't see Owen. He was talking to a female human."

Ah. We all know what happens when male and female humans start talking to each other. They don't pay any attention to the dog.

"And you know humans," Jazzy goes on. "Unless they actually know you, they think all pugs look the same. When it was time to go, the boy thought I was Muffin."

"Well, Kathy must have known you weren't her dog," Shadow says.

"Oh, yes," Jazzy says. "She told

the boy to take me back to the dog park and bring Muffin home. But he said I *was* Muffin. And then he left."

"What did Kathy do?" Shadow asks.

"She tried to find Muffin. She went to the dog park, but Muffin wasn't there. She put up signs, but no one called. She checked the **P-o-U-N-D**. She even called the

police. But they talked to the neighbor boy and they looked at pictures of Muffin, and finally they told Kathy they thought *I was Muffin*."

What a sad story! It's just as sad as Kayla and Dad not coming back for me.

"Well, *you* know where Muffin is," I say. "She's at your house. Why don't you take Kathy there?"

Jazzy looks at me. "Why would I do that?" she asks.

"Because Kathy isn't your human," I say. "You can't keep a human who isn't yours. Besides, Kathy misses Muffin. And Muffin probably misses her. They should be together."

"Yes, but then what will happen to me?" Jazzy asks. "Owen doesn't want me anymore."

"Well..." I think about that for a little bit. Then all of a sudden an idea explodes inside my head. "You can come live with me and Connor and Mom!"

"I can?" Jazzy asks.

"Sure," I say.

I tell Jazzy all about Kayla and Dad and how they went missing. I tell her that I need to go look for them. And I probably need to look for them outside of Four Lakes. But it's hard to do that when I have these new humans to take care of.

"*You* can be Connor and Mom's dog!" I tell Jazzy. "You can take care of them. Then I can go look for Kayla and Dad. And when I find them I can stay with them. I won't have to worry about Connor and Mom."

It's the perfect plan!

"Are Connor and his mom good humans?" Jazzy asks.

"They're great," I say. In fact, they're so great that there's a little voice inside my head asking, *Are you sure you want to leave such nice humans?* But I have to find my other family. I'll do whatever it takes to find them.

"Let me introduce you." I lead Jazzy over to Connor and Mom.

"Hey, guys. This is Jazzy," I say.

"Hi, Buddy. Hi, Jazzy," Connor says.

Jazzy is impressed. "These humans speak Dog?" she asks.

"Not exactly," I say. "But sometimes, like right now, they'll surprise you, and you'll think maybe they do."

"Just like any humans, I guess," Jazzy says, wagging her tail.

Connor reaches into his treat bag and tosses Jazzy and me two liver treats. Like I said: I LOVE liver treats. They're my favorite food!

I think Jazzy likes them, too. "Okay," she says as she gobbles up her treat. "I could live with these humans."

"First we have to get Muffin back to Kathy," I say.

I can tell Kathy misses her dog a lot. Her eyes are all watery, and she's talking in a funny voice.

"I don't know if I'll ever see Muffin

again," Kathy tells Mom. "What happened to her is a real mystery."

Not a mystery, just a problem. And it's a problem that is much easier for dogs to solve than humans. All we have to do is:

🐾 Go to Jazzy's house.

🐾 Help Muffin escape.

🐾 Take Muffin back to Kathy.

🐾 Leave Jazzy with Connor and Mom.

Then I can get back to the real mystery, which is: What happened to my people?

"So when are we going to do all this?" Jazzy asks me.

"Tonight," I say. "After our humans are asleep."

"How?" Jazzy asks. "How will we get out of our houses?"

"Doesn't Kathy have a doggy door?" I ask.

"No," Jazzy says.

Oh. That could be a problem.

"Well, why don't you just tell me how to get to your old house and I'll go get Muffin by myself," I say. "I'll bring her to Kathy's house, and we'll make a lot of noise to wake her up. When she opens the door, you run out. Then I'll bring you to Connor's house."

What could possibly go wrong?

# 3
# Escape

I LOVE nighttime. It's my favorite time!

I hop onto Connor's bed and snuggle up against him. I watch the moon and the stars. I listen to the owls and the crickets. I rest my head on Connor's leg and wait for sleep sounds to come out of his nose.

When I hear Connor's sleep sounds, that's my signal. It's safe to leave the house.

I creep quietly down the stairs
and out through the doggy door. I
smell nighttime all over the grass.

I've never tried to escape from
Connor's yard before. I didn't think
it would be hard. But now that I'm
out here, it's harder than I thought.

That fence is pretty high. It goes
all around the whole yard.

"Mouse?" I call. Mouse is my
friend. He's a dog, not a mouse.
Maybe he can help me escape.

But he doesn't answer. Maybe he
is asleep inside his doghouse?

I follow the fence with my nose.
Flowers … dirt … worm … grass …
rabbit hole … wait, rabbit hole?

No! This is not a good time to
chase rabbits.

The fence jiggles as something leaps onto the top. It's Cat with No Name. He glares down at me.

Cat with No Name and I are not friends.

"Hey!" I cry, lunging at him. "This is my yard. Stay out!"

"Is it *really* your yard?" Cat asks. "I thought that was your yard over there." He tilts his head toward Kayla's dark house.

"Well...," I pause, not sure how to finish that sentence. "They are both my yards."

Cat slowly walks along the top of the fence. I hate that he can jump up there and I can't. I hate that he can walk along the top of the fence and I can't.

"If this is your yard, why are you trying so hard to escape?" Cat asks me. As though it's his business!

"I'm not trying to escape," I say. Lying to cats isn't really lying. "I'm... guarding my yard. I'm making sure no one comes in who isn't supposed to."

"Right," says Cat with No Name. He arches his back and turns around. "Then I guess you don't want me to tell you where the escape is." He jumps down into the Deerbergs' yard on the other side of the fence. Where I can't see him.

"Wait! Come back!" I say, leaping against the fence. I know he can still hear me. "Tell me where the escape is. Tell me! Tell me!"

I hate myself for begging. It doesn't do any good anyway. Cat with No Name is gone.

I wonder if he even told me the truth. I wonder if there really is an escape.

I sniff deeper. Grass…dirt… worm…back to the dirt. Just how soft is this dirt? I paw at it a little. It's pretty soft. I dig deeper…and deeper…and deeper. Now I have a nice-sized hole under the fence between Connor's yard and the Deerbergs' yard next door.

I try and shimmy my way through, but the hole isn't quite big enough. I dig some more. I push with my back paws as well as my front paws. And before I know it, I have broken through

the ground on the other side of the
fence.

"Ha!" I call out to Cat with No
Name. Just in case he's still around.
"I found my own way out!"

"BUDDY?" calls a loud voice from
a few houses away. "BUDDY, IS THAT
YOU?"

I would know that voice anywhere.
"Mouse!"

Mouse is the biggest, loudest dog
on our street. He is charging straight
toward me.

I run to meet him. "It's good to see
you," I say as we greet each other the
dog-fashioned way. "But why did you
call me Buddy? You've always called
me King."

"I CALL YOU WHATEVER

YOUR HUMANS CALL YOU," Mouse
explains. "YOUR OTHER HUMANS
CALLED YOU KING. BUT THESE
HUMANS CALL YOU BUDDY. YOUR
NAME IS BUDDY NOW."

After tonight, Connor and Mom
won't be my humans anymore. They'll
be Jazzy's humans. But Mouse doesn't
know that yet.

"WHAT ARE YOU DOING?"
Mouse asks. "WHY DID YOU DIG
YOUR WAY OUT OF YOUR YARD?"

I tell Mouse all about Jazzy and
Muffin. I tell him I am giving my
humans to Jazzy. "Do you want to
come with me to get Muffin?"

"SURE," Mouse says. He is always
up for an adventure. "LET'S GO!"

Jazzy told me her house was next to

the school. Mouse and I know the way to the school. We have both been there for Take-Your-Pet-to-School Day.

We have to go past Kayla's house to get to the school. I am happy, happy, happy about this because I can sniff Kayla's yard along the way and find out if anything has changed.

It's getting harder to smell Kayla and her dad because it's been so long since they've been here. *Where are they? Why haven't they come home?*

I sniff the driveway … the front flowers … the big yard. People who are not my people have been here. In fact, several people who are not my people have been here.

I stop in front of a square sign in the yard. "Hey, what's this? Where did this come from?" I ask, sniffing all around it. A dog whom I don't know has marked territory here, which makes me a little bit mad. No, wait. It makes me *a lot* mad.

"ARE THERE WORDS ON THAT SIGN?" Mouse asks as he comes up behind me.

It's dark out, so it's hard to tell.

"Of course there are words on it," says a voice from the bushes. Cat with No Name is back. Maybe he never left. Maybe he hid in the bushes and watched me and Mouse. Cats are sneaky that way.

"Would you like to know what the words say?" the cat asks.

I hate that he can

read and I can't.

Don't ask him, I tell myself.
You don't want to owe Cat with No
Name any favors. Don't ask...don't
ask...don't ask...but sometimes my
mouth starts talking all by itself.

"What do they say?" I ask. He
probably won't tell me.

But Cat with No Name surprises
me. "They say: 'For rent.'"

# 4
# A Bad Feeling

"FOR RENT?" Mouse says. "WHAT DOES THAT MEAN?"

"It means his humans aren't coming back," says Cat with No Name. "Ever!" Then he disappears into the night.

My tail droops. Is Cat with No Name right? Are Kayla and her dad never coming back?

What about Mom?

What about all the things inside the house? My toys. The living room couch. All the food Kayla, Mom, and Dad kept hidden behind doors? Are those things still there?

I lumber up the front steps and peer inside the window next to the door. It's just as dark inside the house as it is outside. Lucky for me my eyes work pretty well in the dark.

All I see is a wall with empty hooks. It's the same thing I saw the last time I looked inside my house.

"IF WE'RE GOING TO GET MUFFIN TONIGHT, WE'D BETTER GET GOING," Mouse says. He knows I'd rather go inside my house and look for clues. His quiet voice tells me he will let me be the alpha dog. If I want to go inside my house, we'll try to find a way in. If I would rather go and get Muffin, we'll go and get Muffin.

"We need to stick with the plan," I tell Mouse. "We need to bring Muffin to Kathy, and then we need to bring Jazzy to Connor and his mom. Once I've done all that, *then* I can worry about what happened to my family."

Mouse and I head down the street toward the school. It isn't far. We cross the street at the fire hydrant…turn left at the big rock… turn right at the sidewalk with the fence next to it and follow the sidewalk to the school.

"Hey! Who's there? What do you want? Do you want trouble?"

some little dogs call to us from inside
a house across the street. They look
like toy poodles. I count one … two
of them. I'm pretty sure that's right.
I know "one" and "two." It's all the
numbers that come after two that
are hard.

"We don't want any trouble," I tell
the toy poodles as we walk across the
schoolyard.

"WE'RE JUST HERE TO PICK
SOMEBODY UP AND THEN WE'RE
GOING TO LEAVE," Mouse says.

The little dogs quiet down right
away when they hear Mouse's voice.
That happens a lot when he's around.

"Jazzy's house must be right
around here," I tell Mouse. "She
says it has tomatoes, onions, green

beans, and squash growing in the backyard. She also said to watch out for the squash."

"WHY? WHAT'S SQUASH?" Mouse asks.

"I'm not sure. Jazzy says it's a big smelly plant with flowers so big they could suck your whole head inside them."

"WOW!" Mouse's eyes get big.

But I'm not too worried. If that squash tries anything, Mouse will attack it.

We walk around to the back of the school, our noses twitching in the night air. The schoolyard goes right to a bunch of backyards.

"I SMELL TOMATOES," Mouse says.

I smell them, too. But I don't
smell any of the other stuff yet.
Wait, now I do. Tomatoes... onions...
green beans... and LOOK AT THE
FLOWERS ON THE PLANT IN
THAT YARD OVER THERE. That
must be the squash!

I turn to Mouse. "I think we're
here."

The squash does look a little
scary at night, but it's just a plant.
It's not going to bother us. Mouse
and I walk right past it all the way
into Jazzy's backyard.

"Jazzy said one of the basement
windows has a hole in it," I tell
Mouse. We move closer to the house.
"We might have to make the hole a
little bigger, but we should be able

to get into the house through that window."

There is a window on each side of the back steps. Mouse sniffs at one. I sniff at the other.

"Here it is," I say as my nose pokes through a hole.

It's a good thing no one has clipped my nails recently. I lift my paw and tear the screen all the way across.

There's an inside window, too, but it's not closed all the way. I use my nose to push it open. Now we can get inside the house.

I don't know how far it is to the ground. I hope it isn't very far because HERE ... I ... GO!

Oomph!

I land on something soft. A bed. Good thing there isn't a human in it.

I turn around. "Come on in," I tell Mouse. "It's a soft landing."

Mouse slowly pushes his head through the torn screen. His head and shoulders take up the entire window.

"I DON'T KNOW..." Mouse backs away. "I DON'T THINK I'LL FIT THROUGH THERE."

I'm not sure he will, either, now that I look at him.

"Okay. You wait here," I say. "I'll go get Muffin and come right back."

I blink my eyes to adjust to the darkness, then I jump down from the bed and hurry into the next room. There's a big comfy couch and TV in

here and stairs across the room. I
don't want to wake the humans, so I
tiptoe up the stairs.

I'm a little surprised Muffin
hasn't smelled or heard Mouse and
me. I'm surprised she hasn't come
running to see who we are and what
we want.

But this isn't her house. And
she's probably so upset about being
away from Kathy that she may not
care if there are intruders here.

When I reach the kitchen at the
top of the stairs, I can see how badly
Muffin misses her human. She has
not cleaned up the dried applesauce
on the floor in Jazzy's house. I LOVE
applesauce. It's my favorite food!

And look! There are cracker

crumbs and raisins under that chair. I LOVE cracker crumbs and raisins. They're my favorite foods!

Better check the rest of the kitchen. If Muffin isn't going to clean things up around here, I will.

Sniff... sniff... hey, there's dog food inside this bin. It smells different from mine. I try pushing... I try biting... I can't get the lid off the bin to sample it.

Maybe Muffin left some in Jazzy's bowl?

I look around. That's strange... there are no bowls on the floor for food or water.

Well, maybe these humans don't feed Jazzy (or Muffin) in the kitchen.

I finish cleaning up the kitchen,

then I look around for Muffin. I sniff the living room ... the bathroom ... and while I'm in the bathroom, I pause to take a drink out of the nice big white bowl. Then I continue on to the bedrooms.

I check the first one. No Muffin.

No humans, either. Just a small bed that hasn't been slept in. And a desk with a computer on it.

I check another bedroom. This must be Owen's room. It's got a lot of the same things that Connor has in his room: bed, dresser, soccer ball, kite, pieces for building things. But no human and no dog.

One of the dresser drawers is hanging open. I check it out. It's empty.

I have a bad feeling about this.

I go to the last bedroom. This one smells like a mom and dad's room. Still no humans.

There are no humans or dogs anywhere in this house.

# 5
# Our Problem Becomes a Mystery

"WHAT DO YOU MEAN THERE ARE NO HUMANS OR DOGS ANYWHERE IN THE HOUSE?" Mouse asks when I return to the window. "DID YOU CHECK THE WHOLE HOUSE?"

"Yes." I climb out of the window and shake myself off. "There's nobody here."

"BUT IT'S NIGHTTIME," Mouse

says. "HUMANS ARE ALWAYS IN THEIR BEDS AT NIGHTTIME."

"Not if they've gone away." *Like my humans.*

"IF THEY WENT AWAY, WHERE'S MUFFIN?" Mouse asks.

That's a good question. "I think our problem has just become a mystery," I say.

Mouse plops down on the grass. "SO WHAT DO WE DO NOW? HOW DO WE SOLVE A MYSTERY?"

I've only solved one mystery by myself: the Mystery of the Lost Boy. But I solved it the same way Kayla and I solved mysteries together. I made lists of what I knew, what I didn't know, and what I was going to do to find out what I didn't know.

Here is what I know about this case:
- 🐾 Muffin is not here.
- 🐾 Jazzy's humans are not here, either.
- 🐾 I don't know very much.

Here is what I don't know:
- 🐾 Where did Jazzy's humans go?
- 🐾 Did they take Muffin with them?
- 🐾 Where is Muffin?

Here is what I'm going to do to find out what I don't know:
??? 
"WERE THERE ANY CLUES

INSIDE THE HOUSE?" Mouse asks.

I have to think about that. What did I smell? What did I hear? What did I see?

"There was dog food in the kitchen," I tell Mouse. "But no food or water bowls."

"THAT'S A GOOD CLUE," Mouse says. "THAT MAKES ME THINK THEY TOOK MUFFIN WITH THEM. DID YOU FIND ANY OTHER CLUES?"

"There was an open dresser drawer in Owen's room. It was empty. That might be another clue."

"WHAT DO HUMANS PUT IN DRESSER DRAWERS?" Mouse asks. He is an outdoor dog so I'm not surprised that he doesn't know this.

"Clothes," I say.

"SO WHEREVER THEY WENT, THESE PEOPLE TOOK THEIR CLOTHES WITH THEM," Mouse says. He licks his paw. "DID THEY TAKE ANYTHING ELSE?"

"I don't know," I say. "I've never been inside their house before so I don't know what else is missing. All I know is there's a lot of stuff they *didn't* take."

"THEN THEY'RE PROBABLY COMING BACK," Mouse says. "MAYBE THEY JUST WENT ON A TRIP."

"When humans go on a trip, they sometimes take their dog with them," I say. "But sometimes they don't."

Here is a list of places Muffin could be:

She could be with Jazzy's humans, wherever they are.

 She could be with a neighbor, a friend, or another family member.

She could be at Barker Bob's or another place like it. How many other places like Barker Bob's are there in this town?

She could be at the P-O-U-N-D. I hope she's not!

How do we find out where Muffin is? How do we find more clues?

I know what Kayla would do if she was here. She'd talk to people.

Mouse and I can't do that. Most people don't speak Dog.

But *dogs* speak Dog. We can talk to other dogs and see if they know where Muffin could be.

Mouse and I go back to the house with the two toy poodles. We stand on the sidewalk in front of their house.

"Hello?" I call.

Both dogs come running. "Who's there? What do you want? Are you looking for trouble?" they bark at us.

They have the same kind of window next to their front door as Kayla has. It is such a small window that they are pushing each other

out of the way so they can both see outside.

"No, no. We don't want any trouble," I say. "We just want to know about the dog that lives in the house with the tomatoes, onions, green beans, and squash growing in the backyard. Do you know which house I'm talking about? Do you know the dog that lives there?"

"Sure. We know Jazzy," says the bigger toy poodle.

"We haven't seen Jazzy in a long time," says the smaller toy poodle. "There was another dog there the other day. A dog that isn't Jazzy."

"We know," I say. "That's Muffin. She got mixed up with Jazzy at the dog park. We're here to help Muffin get back home. But Muffin isn't at Jazzy's house. *No one* is there."

"That's because the family went on vacation," the bigger toy poodle says.

"DID THEY TAKE MUFFIN WITH THEM?" Mouse asks.

The toy poodles back away from the window.

"Shh!" I tell Mouse. If his loud voice scares them away, we won't get the information we need.

"Did they take Muffin with them?" I ask in a softer voice.

"No," the smaller toy poodle says. "We saw Grandma come. I think she took Owen and the dog to her house."

*Grandma!* Kayla and her dad went to Grandma's house, too. It's probably not the same Grandma, though. It's probably just another lady named Grandma.

"DO YOU KNOW WHERE THIS GRANDMA LIVES?" Mouse asks. "DOES SHE LIVE AROUND HERE?"

Before the toy poodles can answer, a light comes on inside their house. Then another light comes on above the porch.

"What are you two barking about?" grumbles a voice inside the house.

The front door opens, and a man who doesn't have a lot of hair on his head looks out at us. "Ah," he says. "*That's* what you're barking about." He steps onto the porch. Uh-oh. He's carrying a baseball bat.

# 6
# Does Anyone Smell a River?

"RUN!" the toy poodles warn.

Mouse and I don't need to be told twice. We turn tail and RUN.

"Grandma lives close to the river," one of the toy poodles calls after us. "My human and I went there with Jazzy and her human once. If you can find the river, you'll find Grandma. And, if you find Grandma, you should find Owen and that other dog, too."

"THANKS!" Mouse calls back as we round the corner to the next block.

I glance over my shoulder. "It's okay," I tell Mouse. "The poodle's human isn't following us."

"GOOD!" Mouse says as we slow to a walk. "I DON'T KNOW WHY HE HAD TO COME AFTER US WITH A BASEBALL BAT. WE WERE JUST TALKING TO THOSE DOGS. WE WEREN'T DOING ANYTHING WRONG."

"Some humans don't like it when dogs talk," I say.

"HE STILL DIDN'T HAVE TO GET A BASEBALL BAT," Mouse says.

"Well, if we don't want another human to come after us with a baseball bat, we'd better be quiet," I tell Mouse.

"SORRY," Mouse whispers. We look for cars, then cross the street. "So DO YOU KNOW WHERE THE RIVER IS? I'VE NEVER BEEN THERE."

"Neither have I," I say. "Maybe we can smell it." A river should smell like fish. And boats. And I don't know what else because I've never smelled one.

I don't smell fish... or boats... or anything that might be a river right now.

"MAYBE WE SHOULD ASK FOR DIRECTIONS TO THE RIVER," Mouse says.

"Is there anyone around here who could give us directions?" I ask.

We raise our noses in the air and sniff. We both smell a bunch of different dog smells. Lots of dogs have passed by here. But are any of those dogs still around?

My nose twitches. Yes, there's one who is close. A girl dog. Mouse and I smell her at the exact same time. We both turn our heads. And there, in the window across the street, is not just a girl, but a *lady*. A lady golden retriever. She's the prettiest golden retriever I've ever seen.

I swallow hard. "I wonder if she knows how to get to the river," I ask Mouse.

"THERE'S ONLY ONE WAY TO FIND OUT," Mouse says.

We hurry across the street. "Let

me do the talking," I tell Mouse. "We don't want your loud voice to scare her."

"OKAY," Mouse whispers. He steps aside so I can get to the window first.

My heart is pounding fast, fast, fast. "Hi," I say, just loud enough for the lady to hear me through the glass.

"My name is ... Buddy." That actually isn't such a bad name, now that I think about it.

"I'm Goldy," says the golden retriever. I like the way Goldy slowly blinks her eyes.

I tell Goldy who we are and what we're looking for.

"I haven't been to the river in a long time," Goldy says. "I've got a bad hip."

"That's too bad," I say.

"But I know where the river is," Goldy says. "Just keep going on this street until it ends, then turn toward the hamburger smell. Follow the hamburger smell until it turns into a river smell. You'll know it when you smell it."

"That sounds easy," I say.

"I've heard there's a strange dog hanging around the neighborhood next to the river," Goldy says. "I don't know the name. I don't even know if it's a boy or a girl. But maybe it's your friend."

"DO YOU KNOW ANYTHING ABOUT THE DOG?" Mouse asks. "ANYTHING AT ALL?"

"All I know is he or she is short

and stocky," Goldy says. "And has a pushed-in face."

Pushed-in face? Pugs have pushed-in faces.

"THAT SOUNDS LIKE MUFFIN!" Mouse exclaims.

"Shh!" I hiss.

Mouse says "sorry" with his eyes. He just can't help talking so loud. Especially when he's excited.

But I'm excited, too. Maybe the strange dog *is* Muffin.

"Thanks," I say to Goldy. "Uh... maybe I'll run into you again sometime."

"Maybe," Goldy replies. Then she blinks again, and my whole insides get fluttery.

"YOU LIKE HER, DON'T YOU?"

Mouse teases me when we are away from Goldy's house.

"Sure, I like her," I tell Mouse. I keep my eyes pointed straight ahead. "I like everyone."

Mouse laughs. "YEAH, BUT YOU LIKE HER MORE THAN YOU LIKE MOST DOGS."

"Don't be weird," I tell Mouse. "We've got a mystery to solve."

Mouse and I continue down the street. When we get to the end, I sniff to the left, then sniff to the right. I definitely smell hamburgers to the right. So does Mouse.

We follow the hamburger smell past a bunch of houses... up and down a hill. Goldy was right—the hamburger smell is starting to mix with another smell. Fish... both live fish and dead fish... beavers... boats ... and something else. Is that the smell of river?

"Grandma must live around here somewhere," I say, glancing around the neighborhood. "But where? Which house?"

I don't know if we have time to search each house. It's going to be light soon. Connor's mom gets up as soon as it's light out. I have to be back by then.

"I KNOW HOW TO SPEED THIS UP," Mouse says. He steps back then says in an even louder voice than normal: "HEY! IS ANYONE OUT THERE? WE HEARD THERE WAS A STRANGER HANGING AROUND

HERE. HAS ANYONE SEEN A SHORT, STOCKY STRANGER WITH A PUSHED-IN FACE?"

There is a rustling in the bushes up ahead. A short dog with a pushed-in face steps through the bushes. But it's not Muffin. It's one very angry-looking Shih Tzu.

# 7
# News from Springtown

"PUSHED-IN FACE? SOMEONE
TOLD YOU I HAVE A PUSHED-IN
FACE?"

Wow. This dog is almost as loud
as Mouse! And he isn't anywhere near
as big.

"WHO TOLD YOU THAT?" asks
the Shih Tzu, running a circle around
us. "WHO SAID I HAVE A PUSHED-
IN FACE? I'LL PUSH IN *HIS* FACE!"

Mouse and I look at each other. It's hard to say whether this is the stranger Goldy heard about or not. He *is* short and stocky. And, well ... he does have a sort of pushed-in face. But he's clearly not Muffin.

"Nobody told us *you* have a pushed-in face," I say. "The dog we're looking for has a pushed-in face."

"Who are you looking for?" the Shih Tzu asks. He's calming down a little now. "What's his name? What's your name? My name's Sarge."

"I'm ... Buddy." The more I say it, the more I believe it is my name. "This is my friend, Mouse."

"Hi, Buddy. Hi, Mouse." Sarge lifts his paw. "You guys aren't from around here either, are you? Where are you from? I'm from Springtown."

*Springtown?* That catches my
attention. That's where Kayla's
grandma lives. It's where Kayla and
her dad went when they left me at
Barker Bob's.

"Are you from there, too?" Sarge
asks. "Did you get caught in the
tornado?"

Tornado? "There was a tornado in
Springtown?" I ask.

"Yes," Sarge replies. "Have you
ever been in a tornado? The one that
went through Springtown was the
loudest, scariest thing I ever heard.
It sounded like a freight train, but it
was really a big, swirling cloud. Big
as our whole block. It roared through
the town and picked up cars, trees,

even houses and threw them down
like they were nothing."

"THAT SOUNDS TERRIBLE,"
Mouse says.

I agree. I've seen tornados on TV,
but I've never seen one in real life.

"Was it a really bad tornado? Did

anyone...you know?" I ask.

Mouse moves closer to me.
"YOU'D KNOW IF YOUR HUMANS
DIED," he says. "YOU'D FEEL IT."

He's right, of course. And I don't
feel as though Kayla and Dad...I
can't say the word. I can't even think

it. But I know *something* bad has happened to my humans. That's what I feel.

"I don't think anyone died," Sarge says. "But the town is in bad shape. A lot of humans lost their houses. Including my humans. There were dogs and cats wandering around town without any food, water, or a place to sleep. It was awful."

"WHAT HAPPENED?" Mouse asks. "HOW DID YOU GET HERE?"

"The dogcatchers came," Sarge says. "They caught a lot of us. They lured us with food and water. Then they put us on trucks and drove us to different towns. I was one of the lucky ones. I escaped from the truck. I don't know what happened to the dogs who didn't escape."

I wonder if they ended up at the **P-o-U-N-D**. I didn't talk to anyone from Springtown when I was there. And I didn't hear about any tornado. But the **P-o-U-N-D** is a big place. I certainly didn't talk to everyone.

"So, what do you know about Springtown?" Sarge asks me.

I tell him about my humans. My old humans.

If they got caught in the tornado, that would explain why they never came back.

"Do you know the way to Springtown?" I ask Sarge. "Can you take me there?" All I have to do is bring Muffin to Kathy, bring Jazzy to Connor and Mom, and then I will be ready to go.

Sarge shakes his head. "It's too dangerous to go back there right now."

Too dangerous? What kind of dog lets a little danger stand between him and his humans?

"My humans could be hurt," I say. "They could be hurt bad. I have to go to them. I have to help."

"If they're hurt, you won't be able to go to them," Sarge tells me. "Not if they're in a hospital. Dogs aren't allowed in hospitals. You'll probably get picked up by a dogcatcher if you try to go in. And if you get picked up by a dogcatcher, you could end up anywhere. How are you going to help your humans then?"

"IF YOU GET PICKED UP BY A

DOGCATCHER IN SPRINGTOWN, YOU MIGHT NEVER SEE YOUR OLD PEOPLE *OR* YOUR NEW PEOPLE AGAIN!" Mouse cries.

That would be bad.

I drop to the ground. The grass feels wet against my belly. *I don't know what to do!* I want to go to Springtown. But I don't want to get picked up by a dogcatcher and taken to a strange town.

"Will you go back to Springtown someday?" I ask Sarge.

"Sure. As soon as it's safe to go back," Sarge says.

"How will you know when it's safe?" I ask.

"I'll check the Network," he says.

The Network is how dogs talk

to each other and get news. One dog sends a message to another dog, who sends a message to another dog, who sends a message to more dogs.

"Until then, this isn't a bad place to hang out," Sarge says. "It's easier to hide from the dogcatcher here than it is in Springtown. I've got a bed in those bushes over there. Sometimes people come along and feed me. And there's water on the other side of those houses."

River water?

"Wouldn't you rather live in a house?" I ask. "With humans?" Maybe he could come back with me and Jazzy and live with Connor and Mom, too. Especially if it's just for a little while.

Then, when it's safe, Sarge and I can go to Springtown together.

"No, I actually prefer to be outdoors now," Sarge says. "That way I'll know if a tornado is coming."

That doesn't sound like a very good life to me.

"I KNOW WHAT YOU'RE THINKING, BUDDY," Mouse says. "BUT REMEMBER, I'M AN OUT-DOOR DOG. IT'S NOT SO BAD. I KIND OF LIKE THE FREEDOM."

"So do I," Sarge says. "But I'll still be happy to see my people again."

The sky is growing lighter. You can hardly see the stars anymore.

Mouse yawns. "YOU KNOW," he says. "IF WE'RE GOING TO FIND YOUR FRIEND TONIGHT, WE

DON'T HAVE MUCH TIME."

Mouse is right. If we're not back soon, our humans will probably call the dogcatcher on *us.*

It's hard to think about Muffin and Jazzy when I just got one step closer to finding out what happened to my humans. But I don't want to go to Springtown and get caught by a dogcatcher.

I can't solve the case of my missing people right now, but I can solve the Case of the Mixed-Up Mutts.

"Let's find Muffin," I tell Mouse. "She must be close."

"Who's Muffin?" Sarge asks.

I give him the short version of what happened with Muffin and Jazzy. "Have you seen a pug anywhere around here?" I ask.

"Pug?" Sarge says. "Now *that's*
a dog with a pushed-in face. Hey, I
think there's a pug in the house that
smells like oatmeal cookies."

"I LOVE oatmeal cookies," I say.
"They're my favorite food!"

"Mine, too," Sarge says. "I
haven't met that dog. She hasn't
been at that house very long. But if
she's the dog you're looking for, she
might not want to go back to her
humans. Not if there are oatmeal
cookies at her new house."

"I think she'll want to go back,"
I say. Who wouldn't give up cookies
for their real humans?

But I could be wrong.

# 8
# The House That Smells Like Oatmeal Cookies

It's easy to find the house that smells like oatmeal cookies. Mouse and I could probably find it with our noses closed.

There are one … two … eleven … four … six steps leading to a wide front porch. Mouse and I climb the steps and pad over to the big front window.

We peer inside.

I see a pug curled up on a chair next to the fireplace.

I tap my paw against the window. "Hello?" I say. "Are you Muffin?"

The pug looks up. She climbs down from the chair, stretches, and waddles over to us. "How do you know my name?" she asks.

*Yes! She* is *Muffin!*

I tell Muffin who Mouse and I are and why we are here.

"You met Jazzy?" Muffin leaps against the window sill. "And you know my human? How did you find me? This isn't Jazzy's house. This is the grandma's house. Grandma is taking care of me and Owen while Owen's parents are on vacation."

"WE KNOW," Mouse says. "AND

BELIEVE ME, IT WASN'T EASY TO FIND YOU!"

"You have to get me out of here," Muffin says. She spins in several circles. "You have to break me out of this house. You have to take me to my human, and then bring Jazzy back here."

*Bring Jazzy back?* "But Jazzy doesn't want to come back," I say.

Muffin stops spinning. "Why not?"

"She says Owen was the one who switched you guys at the dog park. She says he did it *on purpose*. I came here to bring you back to Kathy. Jazzy is going to come live with my humans. The humans I'm living with now, I mean. Then I'm going to go back to my old humans."

That's the Plan!

"It's true. Owen did switch Jazzy and me," Muffin says. "But he feels really bad about that now."

"He does?" I gulp.

"Yes," Muffin says. "He misses Jazzy a lot. He wants her back."

Hmm. I wonder how Jazzy would feel if she knew that?

"Apparently there's something about the way I cuddle that's wrong," Muffin goes on. "But hey, he's not my human. I only snuggle with my own human, you know?"

"ME, TOO," Mouse says.

I look at Mouse and try to imagine him snuggling with his humans. Without crushing them, I mean.

"Do you have a plan for getting me out of here?" Muffin asks. "Are you going to break the window? Are you going to bring me out through the chimney?"

How would we bring her out through the chimney? I wonder.

At Jazzy's house we just found a hole that was already there and made it a little bigger.

"Are there any holes in the window screens at this house?" I ask Muffin. That would be the easiest way to get her out.

"No." Muffin shakes her head. "I've checked."

"HOW ABOUT A DOGGY DOOR?" Mouse asks.

"No doggy door, either," Muffin says.

"Then I don't know how we're going to get you out of this house," I say.

"You *have* to get me out!" Muffin says. She leaps against the window sill again. "Owen's mom and dad don't know that he switched us. They were too busy packing for their trip when Owen brought me home. But once they actually look at me, they'll know I'm not Jazzy. And I don't know what they'll do with me then. They may take me to the **P-o-U-N-D** and then I'll never see Kathy again."

"WE WON'T LET THAT HAPPEN. WILL WE, BUDDY?" Mouse asks.

"No," I say. "We'll find a way to switch you guys back."

*Somehow.*

"But ... I don't think we're going to be able to do it now," I say.

The sun is just starting to peek over the horizon. I hate to leave Muffin here, but Mouse and I have to go home.

"What? You're not going to leave me here are you?" Muffin cries. "You *can't* leave me here!"

"It's just for a little while," I promise. "We need to figure out how to get you out of here. And, I want to tell Jazzy what you said about Owen wanting him back."

Jazzy might change her mind about moving in with Connor and Mom. Then there will be no dog to take care of Connor and Mom when I go to Springtown to find my family.

But I can't worry about that now. Every dog belongs with their own humans. If Jazzy wants to go home, I have to help her get there.

Unfortunately, finding out what Jazzy wants is harder than I expected it would be.

I thought Mom and Connor would take me back to obedience school. I thought I would see Jazzy there and tell her what Muffin told me.

But day becomes night. And then night becomes day. And day becomes night. And night becomes day. That keeps happening for eleventy-twelve days. I wonder if we are *ever* going back to obedience school.

Will I ever see Jazzy again? Will she and Muffin ever find a way to switch back?

Then one day, when I'm not expecting it, Mom calls, "Buddy! It's time to go to obedience school."

Oh, boy! We *are* going back. I will see Jazzy again. I'm a happy, happy dog.

But there is a problem when we get to obedience school.

Jazzy isn't here.

Class starts, and Jazzy still isn't here. Did Kathy decide not to come? How will I ever find Jazzy?

Today we are working on teaching the humans how to walk nicely. Without pulling on the leash. This is hard for some humans. I don't know why.

While we are walking 'round and 'round and 'round the circle, the door opens. Jazzy and Kathy walk in.

"Jazzy!" I say. "I'm really happy to see you!"

"Buddy, heel!" Mom says, giving my leash a gentle tug.

See what I mean about this being hard for some humans? Even Mom has a hard time not pulling on the leash. But she'll get the hang of it. I know she will.

Jazzy and Kathy look for an opening in our circle. I try to slow Mom down so Jazzy and Kathy can join the circle in front of us. But Mom pulls on the leash again.

There is a bigger opening in the circle between Ike and Rosie. Jazzy and Kathy go over there.

"Jazzy, I've got some good news," I call across the circle. "I found Muffin! She says your human is sorry he switched you and Muffin. He misses you. He wants you back."

"Jazzy! That's great! We're so happy for you," the other dogs cheer.

We all stop walking and sit beside our humans.

"I don't believe you," Jazzy says. She turns her head away from me.

"It's true. You can ask my friend Mouse if you don't believe me. He heard it, too."

Jazzy turns one eye back to me. "Really? Are you sure? Does Owen really want me back?"

"Yes," I say.

"Then I should go back," Jazzy says.

I agree. "The only problem is I don't know how to get you back to Owen and get Muffin back to Kathy. You can't get out at night. And neither can Muffin. She's not even at your house. She's at Owen's grandma's house."

"Can you meet at the dog park some afternoon and switch back then?" Ike asks. "That's where you got switched in the first place."

"I don't know. Kathy doesn't take me to the dog park very often," Jazzy says.

"And," I point out, "there's no

way to tell Kathy and Owen to take you both to the dog park at the same time because..."

"—humans don't speak Dog," all the dogs in class say at the same time.

We all spend the rest of the class thinking about ways to switch Muffin and Jazzy back. But no one comes up with anything until the very end of class.

Then Jazzy says, "I know how we can switch back."

"How?" I ask.

"Wait until the door opens and everyone starts to leave," Jazzy says. "Then follow me."

"What are you going to do, Jazzy?" I ask.

Jazzy doesn't answer.

"Jazzy?" I say again.

But Jazzy turns her back to me.

Whatever Jazzy has planned, I have a feeling I'm not going to like it.

# 9
# On the Run

Jazzy's eyes are fixed on Kathy. She's trying extra hard to make Kathy hold the leash loose as they walk around the circle.

"You're not going to run away from Kathy when class is over, are you?" I ask Jazzy. I'm afraid that's exactly what she's planning. Why else would she say wait until the door opens?

I think of all the bad things that could happen if Jazzy runs away. She could get hit by a car. She could get caught by the dog catcher. She could end up at the **P-o-U-N-D**.

And if I follow Jazzy, all those things could happen to me, too.

"We'll see you next week," the alpha human says.

The humans start gathering up their water bowls and treat bags. Kathy still has a pretty loose hold on Jazzy. Even looser than the hold Connor has on me.

All the dogs are watching Jazzy and me.

"Are you ready?" Jazzy asks.

"Jazzy, listen to me," I say. "There's got to be another way."

"I don't know what it is," Jazzy says.

The door opens and Jazzy jerks her leash out of Kathy's grasp.

"Peaches!" Kathy calls, lunging for the leash.

*Peaches?* Is that what Kathy calls Jazzy?

Jazzy darts through an Irish setter's legs and is out the door.

"Don't let Jazzy go by herself!" the other dogs urge me on. "You have to go with her. You have to help Jazzy find Owen, and you have to help Muffin get back to Kathy!"

They're right. I don't know if Muffin could find her way back to Kathy by herself. I don't even know if I can find Kathy once Muffin and I leave Owen's grandma's house. But I can take Muffin back to Connor and

Mom's house. And then together we can figure out how to find Kathy.

"I have to go," I tell Connor. He is the one who is most likely to understand me. "But don't worry. I'll be back." I pull my leash out of Connor's grasp and make tracks for the door.

"Buddy!" Connor exclaims. "What are you doing?"

Connor starts to run after me, but he's too slow. "Mom!" he screams. "Can you grab Buddy?"

"Go, Buddy!" the other dogs shout. "Don't look back! We won't let your humans catch you." They all move in between Mom and me.

"Somebody, grab Buddy!" Mom cries.

But I am already out the door after Jazzy.

Jazzy glances over her shoulder as I catch up to her. "Hey, this is kind of fun," she giggles. "I've never run away before." She skips into the street.

"JAZZY!" I scream as a car swerves around her. "BE CAREFUL!"

"BUDDY! COME BACK HERE!" Mom yells. I feel her feet pounding on the pavement behind me.

There is an opening in the traffic. I feel bad about running away from Mom, but I have to. I have to follow Jazzy.

"This way!" I tell Jazzy. I tilt my head toward a different street. There are houses over there.

Jazzy slows to look at me. "Is Grandma's house that way?"

"I don't know. I don't think so," I say. "But we have to lose all those humans that are chasing us before we can look for Grandma's house. I think we can do that if we run through those backyards over there."

"Okay," Jazzy says.

"Look for cars this time," I warn her.

We look both ways, then dart across the street...across somebody's front yard, and around to the back. I hope there isn't a fence back there.

There isn't.

Jazzy and I keep running.

Through backyards. Over and around fences. Back to a front yard. Across another street.

I put my nose to the ground. "Hey, I think we drove on this street to get to obedience school," I tell Jazzy. I'm pretty sure I smell Mom and Connor's car.

Jazzy sniffs the edge of the street. "I think I smell it, too."

And we seem to have lost the humans. For now, anyway.

We follow the car trail back to Connor's house.

We pass Mouse's house along the way. He is resting under the big maple tree in his front yard.

"Mouse!" I call to him. "Look who I found."

Mouse raises his head. "HEY … IS THAT JAZZY?" He comes to greet us at the fence.

"Yes, it is!" I say as we hurry on past.

"Nice … to … meet you … Mouse," Jazzy puffs. She's getting tired, I can tell.

We can't slow down, though. "No time to chat," I tell Mouse over my shoulder. "But guess what? I'm taking Jazzy home!"

"THAT'S GREAT," Mouse calls back. "BUT THEN WHO'S GOING TO MOVE IN WITH CONNOR AND MOM WHEN YOU GO TO SPRINGTOWN?"

I can't think about that right now.
The trail Mouse and I left when we
came back from Owen's grandma's
house should be around here somewhere. If I can find it, we should be
able to follow it in reverse.

"I have to get Jazzy back to her
house before the humans catch us," I
tell Mouse.

I sniff. Ah! There it is!

"Switch to this trail," I tell Jazzy.

We follow the new trail up one
street and down another. For some
reason it doesn't take as long to find
Jazzy's house now as it took us to
come back the other morning. But
that's probably because we have a
trail to follow.

"We're getting close," Jazzy says,

speeding up. "I smell Grandma. I smell Owen, too!"

I smell Muffin!

We round another corner and there, up ahead, is Owen's grandma's house. Muffin is outside. She's sitting on the top step of the porch with Owen.

They both turn to look at us.

"Jazzy?" Owen says, his eyes growing wide. He rises to his feet. "Is it really you?"

# 10
# A Happy Ending

Owen leads Muffin down the stairs. He bends down in front of Jazzy, and Jazzy licks his ears.

Owen giggles. "It *is* you. Isn't it, girl?"

"Of course it's me," Jazzy says, wagging her whole back end.

"You came back," Muffin says as she circles me. Her tail is going about a million miles an hour. "And you brought Jazzy with you. Now we can switch back."

"That's the plan," I say.

"How did you ever find your way back, Jazzy?" Owen asks. He hugs Jazzy again. "I'm really sorry I took the wrong dog that other day. I don't know what I was thinking."

"I forgive you," Jazzy says.

"Yeah, yeah," Muffin says. "Now what about me? Are you going to take me to my human?"

The door to the house opens and an older female human steps outside.

"Owen?" she says as she marches down the stairs. She's got a leash in one hand. "What's going on? Where did all these dogs come from?"

"I don't know, Grandma," Owen

says, rubbing Jazzy's back. "They just showed up."

Grandma looks from Jazzy to Muffin and back again. "You'd better put a leash on Jazzy." She holds the leash out to Owen. "Do you know which one is Jazzy? Those two look exactly alike."

"To you, maybe," Jazzy says with a sniff. "Not to us."

"This one is Jazzy," Owen says, picking her up.

Grandma rubs her chin. "Are you sure? Do they have tags?"

Owen crosses his fingers behind his back. "I don't know what happened to Jazzy's tags," he says in a low voice. "I think we lost them."

*He's lying!* A dog can always tell

when a human isn't telling the truth. Jazzy told me what happened to the tags she and Muffin were wearing that day at the dog park.

"Well, what about the other dog?" Grandma reaches toward Muffin, but Muffin pulls away. She isn't wearing any tags, either.

"We'd better go," Muffin says.

I agree. We don't want Grandma to call the dog catcher. "I'm glad you're back with your human, Jazzy," I say. "Let's go, Muffin!"

As I turn to head back down the sidewalk, Mom's car pulls to a stop in front of Jazzy's house. Mom and Kathy get out of the front doors. Connor gets out the back.

How did they know where Jazzy

and I went?

"Buddy!" Connor cries, racing toward me.

"MOM!" Muffin cries, racing toward Kathy. She runs straight into Kathy's arms.

I let Connor hug me. "How did you find me?" I ask. But he doesn't answer. He just keeps hugging me.

"Are these your dogs?" Grandma asks Mom and Kathy.

"Yes," Mom says. "I'm sorry they're running loose. They got away from us at the end of…" she pauses. "Obedience class."

"Well, two of them did," Kathy says. "Yours and hers." She points to Mom. "My dog has been here for the last two and a half weeks."

Grandma's mouth drops open. "I beg your pardon."

"Our dogs got switched. At the dog park," Kathy explains. "But it's okay. This one is mine. And I can tell by the way your boy is petting that one she must be his."

"How did all these dogs end up here?" Grandma asks. "And how did you know they were here?"

"We didn't," Mom says. "We just started driving around."

"*I* told Mom to go this way," Connor says. "I saw Buddy running, and I thought he might be heading toward the river."

"I don't know how you knew that," Mom says.

"Me, either." Connor shrugs.

"It doesn't matter how we got here," Kathy says. "The important thing is we did. Can we take our dogs home now?"

"I don't know," Grandma says, scratching her head. "Maybe we should wait until my daughter and her husband get home to help us sort all this out. They've been in Europe for the last couple of weeks. That's why Owen and his dog are here with me. I would hate to see them go home with the wrong dog."

"But I know this is my dog," says Owen as Jazzy licks his face.

"And I know this is *my* dog," Kathy says, hugging Muffin closer.

"*How* do you know?" Grandma asks. "Neither dog has any identification.

And they look the same."

"They don't look *exactly* the same," Kathy says. "There's more black around Muffin's nose."

"And there's more white on Jazzy's stomach fur," Owen pipes in.

Grandma adjusts her glasses and takes a closer look at each dog. "I'm sorry," she says. "They look the same to me."

Humans are so limited by what they can see. It's true that Muffin and Jazzy look a lot alike. But they don't smell anything alike.

Finally Kathy says, "I think I know how we can settle this. Is your dog by any chance microchipped?"

"Yes." Owen nods.

"I am?" Jazzy asks. "I don't

remember getting 'microchipped.'"

"It probably happened when you were young," Muffin says.

"My dog is microchipped, too," Kathy says. "All we have to do is find someone to scan the chips."

"What chips?" Connor asks. "What does microchipped mean?"

"It means both our dogs have little computer chips in their shoulders," Owen explains. "A vet can scan a chip and find out whose dog it is. You'll be glad you did it if your dog ever gets lost. Almost any vet can do it."

"Well, what are we waiting for?" Grandma asks. "Let's get in the car and go see your vet."

"This dog's name is Muffin," the vet says. He holds up Muffin's leash. "She's owned by a Kathy Turner, who lives at 308 Park Drive."

Technically, Kathy Turner is owned by a dog named Muffin, but humans never get that right.

"I knew this was my Muffin," Kathy says. She takes the leash from the vet.

"And this is Jazzy," the vet says, handing Jazzy over to Owen and his grandma.

"Jazzy is *my* dog!" Owen says happily.

I LOVE happy endings. But I *don't* love vets. "Let's go," I tell Mom as I pull toward the door.

But Mom isn't in any hurry to

leave. "I wonder if we should have Buddy microchipped," she says out of the blue. "We've had some problems with him running away from us."

I swallow hard. *You want to have me microchipped?*

"Don't worry, Buddy," Jazzy says. "It doesn't hurt a bit."

I'm not worried about pain. A microchip proves who belongs to you when there are no tags. The microchips inside of Muffin and Jazzy proved that Kathy belongs to Muffin and Owen belongs to Jazzy.

If I get a microchip, who will it say belongs to me? Kayla and her mom and dad? Connor and his mom?

I think I know the answer to that question.

"Yeah, let's get Buddy microchipped," Connor says.

"We recommend microchipping for every dog and cat," the vet says.

"Okay, then let's do it!" Mom says.

"Wait a minute! Don't I get a say in this?" I ask.

"Don't you want to be microchipped?" Muffin asks. "Your people seem like really good people. And they must love you a lot if they want to do this. That means they don't want ever to lose you."

"But what about Kayla and her mom and dad?" I say.

"What about them?" Jazzy asks.

I don't answer out loud. But inside, I'm wondering why didn't *they* have me microchipped.

Will I ever know? Will I ever see Kayla, Mom, and Dad again?

I can't leave Connor and his mom. Not unless I find another dog to take care of them. And I wouldn't leave them with just any dog. It would have to be the right dog. One who would take extra good care of them.

If Sarge goes back to Springtown, he will have to go without me.

I'm pretty lucky to have found Connor and mom. They're good people. Just because you have a second family doesn't necessarily mean you forget your first family.

And it doesn't mean you love them any less.

I still don't know whether a dog can *have* two families or not. But a dog can definitely *love* two families.

"All right," I say. "You can microchip me."

The vet takes my leash and leads me down the hall.

"Hey!" Connor calls after us. "Is it going to hurt him when you put the microchip in?"

The vet stops and turns. "No. But you can come along if you want. It won't take very long."

Connor grins and hurries after us.

"Now you'll never get lost, Buddy," Connor says, patting my ribs.

*Buddy.* That name is really starting to grow on me.

I lick his leg. It's nice to love and to be loved.

We go into another room and the vet closes the door behind us.

Jazzy is right. It doesn't hurt when the vet puts this chip inside me. I just feel a little pinch, and then it's over.

Now it's official. I belong to Connor and his mom.

Forever?